For Ryan Alexander Campbell and his big strong heart
—S.G.

Visit us on the Web! randomhousekids.com

Educators and librarians, for a variety of teaching tools, visit us at RHTeachersLibrarians.com

Library of Congress Cataloging-in-Publication Data
Gillingham, Sara, author, illustrator.
How to mend a heart / Sara Gillingham. — First edition.
pages cm.
Summary: Provides friendship advice using sewing metaphors.
ISBN 978-0-553-51093-5 (hardcover) — ISBN 978-0-375-97427-4 (hardcover library binding) — ISBN 978-0-553-51094-2 (ebook)
[1. Friendship—Fiction. 2. Compassion—Fiction.] I. Title.
PZ7.G41554Hp 2015 [E]—dc23 2014047221

Book design by John Sazaklis

MANUFACTURED IN CHINA

10 9 8 7 6 5 4 3 2 1

First Edition

How to Mend a Heart

by Sara Gillingham

Random House 🏠 New York

To mend a heart,

you need gentle hands,

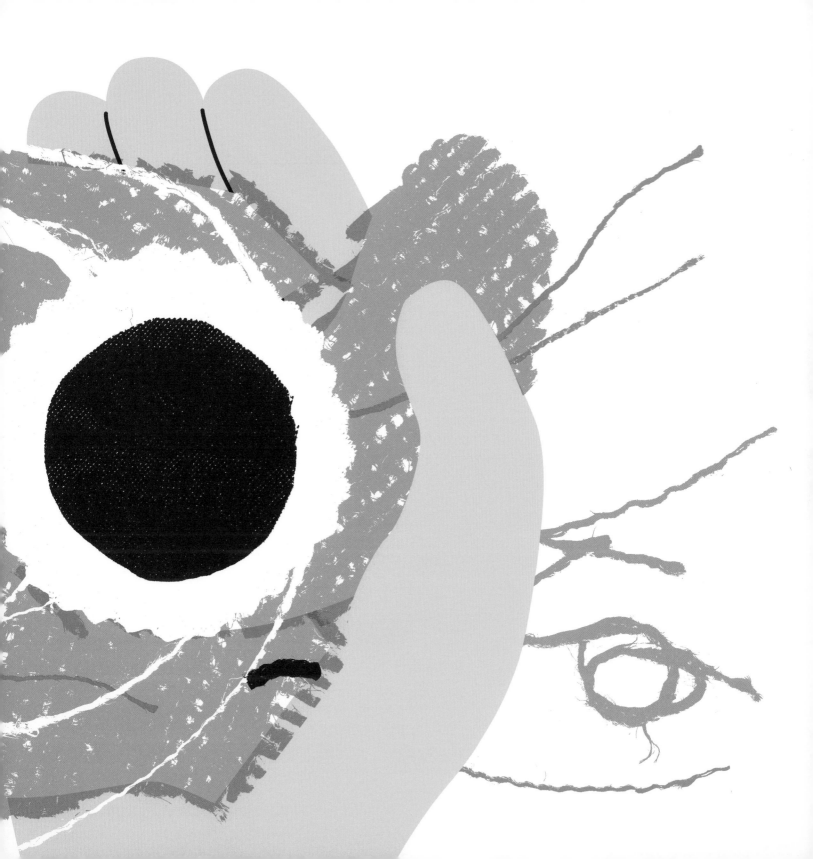

the right tools,

and lots of patches.

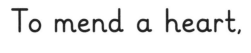

To mend a heart,

go one stitch at a time.

Some hearts need a little bit of thread,

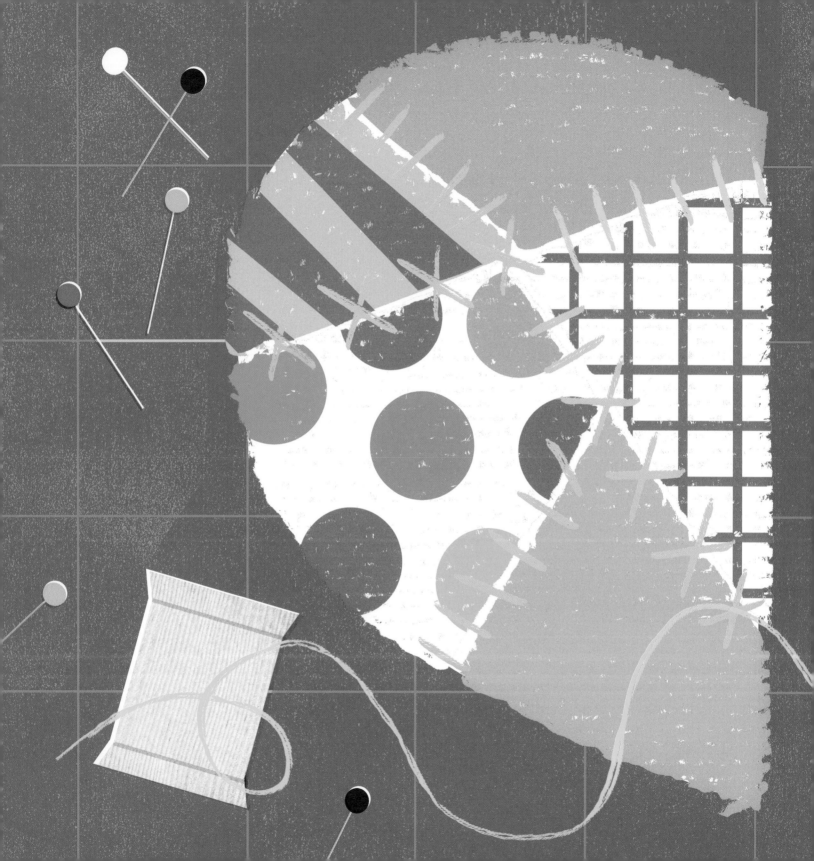

and others need
the whole spool.

If there is a snag,

remember there are

helping hands . . .

all around you.

You might mend a heart
more than once . . .

. . . or twice.

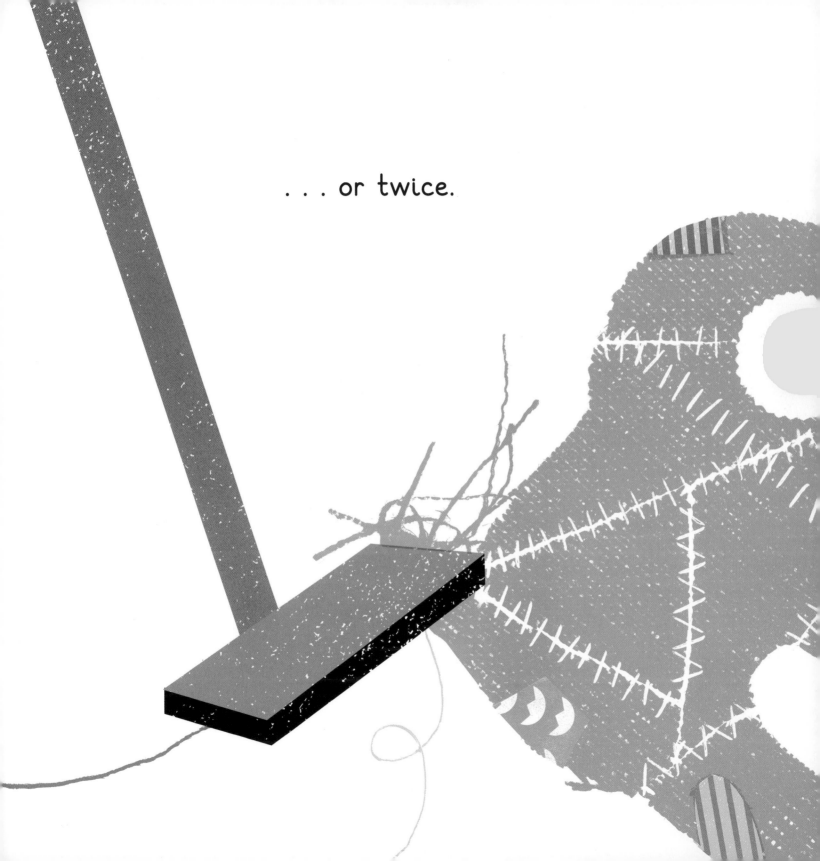

So trim the loose threads,

try something new,

and don't give up,

because the
more patches and
seams there are . . .

the bigger
and stronger

a heart can be.